LITTLE
PENGUiN
RESCUE

STRIPES PUBLISHING LIMITED
An imprint of the Little Tiger Group
1 Coda Studios, 189 Munster Road, London SW6 6AW

A paperback original
First published in Great Britain in 2019

ISBN: 978-1-78895-078-7

Printed and bound in the UK.

2 4 6 8 10 9 7 5 3 1

LITTLE
PENGUIN
RESCUE

Rachel Delahaye

stripes

For Elise and Fleur, who love birds of all feathers
– Rachel

CONTENTS

Cold Play

"It's snowing! It's snowing!" Ella was shouting so loudly that Fliss had to hold the phone away from her ear. "This is the best day of my life!"

"You said that last time it snowed!" Fliss replied, watching the thick flakes falling outside the window.

"Yes, but this snow day is going to be the best. We're going to toboggan down the road and throw snowballs in the garden and drink hot chocolate."

"And get wet bottoms again?" Fliss giggled, remembering how last time they had slipped off their plastic-bag toboggans and skidded down the road laughing.

"Maybe not that," said Ella. "But all the rest of it, definitely! I'll be over as soon as I've had breakfast."

"OK, see you soon!"

Fliss grinned as she put down the phone and pulled on her coat, gloves and boots. She couldn't wait to tell her neighbours, Kamal and Alisha, that Ella was on her way. They could all have a massive snowball fight!

When she opened the back door, the cold hit her face with an icy blast. She blinked away the snowflakes and stepped out into a world she hardly recognized. It was as if a huge white blanket had been thrown over everything. Thick snow had settled on the tops of the fences. Tree branches bowed under its weight. Smaller bushes were completely covered, so they looked like strange, lumpy white monsters.

Fliss hoped all the wild animals had found somewhere safe and warm to stay, because apart from the crunch of her footsteps on the fresh snow, there was no sound. It was all so peaceful. Almost too peaceful… Just a few minutes ago she had heard Kamal and Alisha screaming and laughing outside. Where were they now?

"Hey, Felicity!"

It was Kamal. He always called her by her full name.

"I've told you before – friends call me Fliss!" she said, still unable to see him.

"We're not friends," came the reply. "Not when we're having a snowball fight!"

Suddenly – *WHOOSH!* – a snowball whizzed past Fliss's head. It was an ambush! Kamal and Alisha had been hiding all this time, waiting for her to step outside. Fliss shrieked and ducked as another one flew by.

"Hey! Stop a minute!" she called. Two faces peered over the fence. Fliss quickly scooped up a snowball and threw it back at them. It broke apart in mid-air and showered snow over their heads.

Kamal's eyes twinkled with excitement. There was snow on his nose.

"That's it!" he grinned. "I'm really going to get you now! Come on, Alisha, make as many snowballs as you can. We're going to win this fight."

"Ella's coming over soon. You'll be in trouble then!" Fliss shouted.

"We'll be two against two," said Alisha. Pretty white flakes decorated her dark hair. "That will make it even."

"It'll be nowhere near even. Ella fights like an angry yeti!" laughed Fliss.

While she had been chatting to Alisha, Fliss hadn't noticed Kamal picking up two more snowballs. They flew at her now, one hitting her ear.

"Oh, sorry, Fliss, did I get you?"

Kamal grinned naughtily.

"Yes, you did," Fliss said, pretending to be grumpy. "And I don't like being wet and cold."

"I thought you wanted to be a vet when you grow up?"

"What's that got to do with being hit by a snowball?" asked Fliss.

"Well, vets have to go out in all kinds of weather. If you can't take a bit of snow, I'm not sure you'll cope with being a vet."

Fliss wanted to be a vet more than anything and Kamal knew that. He was smiling, waiting for her reaction.

"I can take snow," she said boldly.

"Take this then!" said Alisha, throwing a snowball that hit her on the forehead.

Fliss calmly wiped the drips from her eyes and held up her hand. "Wait right there," she said.

"What for?" asked Alisha.

"I need my vet equipment to sort out a couple of wild animals – you!" Fliss laughed and ran to the shed at the bottom of the garden. She planned to get a shovel and a bucket so she could collect loads of snow and tip it over the fence and onto their heads.

Inside she found what she needed. She also found a fishing net, which would be perfect for catching snowballs and flinging them back – that would surprise them! Laughing to herself, she opened the door, ready to do battle.

A huge gust of wind forced Fliss to close her eyes. When she opened them, she saw snow-topped black mountains in the distance, glistening beneath the sun, and a steel-blue sea littered with what looked like scrunched-up tissues. Fliss's face tingled and it was so icy cold that it took her breath away. She didn't know where she was – only that she was a long way from home. Freezing and a little frightened, Fliss went back inside the shed and closed the door.

The Shed

When Fliss had got over her shock,
she looked around and saw that the
shed was no longer filled with plastic
plant pots and Dad's rusty tools. It
wasn't made of wood any more and it
definitely wasn't small.

She saw that she was in a hallway
with a plastic floor. She walked down
it, pushed open a heavy door and found
herself in a large, brightly lit room.
There were rugs on the floor and several

large sofas. She spotted some binoculars in the corner and put a pair around her neck. Doors led to other rooms and there were small round windows looking out at the sea.

Where on earth was she? Fliss put down her bucket and fishing net and started to examine a long desk that held several computers. The machines were on and blinked with information. The first one had a document open on the screen. It read:

The New Captain Scott Research Station.

Survey to measure the effects of rising temperatures on the pack ice of Ross Island, Antarctica.

Antarctica! She really *was* far from home. She was at the South Pole!

And those things that looked like scrunched-up tissues – they were icebergs! *This building must be where the scientists live and work*, Fliss thought as she looked around her. Although there was nobody here now. Maybe the scientists were out on the ice, taking their measurements.

Fliss's fear melted away as her attention
was drawn to a map on the wall, showing
Ross Island. Most of the island was white
and it had very few landmarks – just the
names of mountains and peaks, and dots
to show the location of various buildings.
There weren't many: there was a black dot
on the west of the island marked
"Shackleton's Hut" and – aha! – a red dot
below, which meant "you are here". It
showed she was inside The New Captain
Scott Research Station. Right next door
was another dot: "Captain Scott's Hut".

Fliss gasped as she absorbed the
information. Shackleton was a famous
explorer; Captain Scott was even more
famous. He made it to the South Pole two
years before Shackleton. They had trekked
all this way just to see if it was possible.

But why had *she* come all this way?

Well, she wouldn't find out by just sitting around. She knew that the special thing about the South Pole was its landscape, which had hardly been touched by humans. She needed to get out there and see it for herself! Fliss shivered as she remembered the icy blast that had frozen her skin. She was going to need protection.

She looked around and found a wardrobe full of all-in-one suits, glasses, gloves and hats. They were too big for her but she took the smallest-looking suit and slipped it on over her clothes. Then she took a pair of gloves, snow goggles and a beanie hat. She felt like a spaceman crossed with a giant marshmallow, but it would do for now.

The Shed

Fliss opened the door to the outside and the wind whipped round her ears, whistling loudly. She pulled down her hat, snuggled her face inside the top of her snowsuit and looked about. She was high off the ground! She hadn't realized the building was raised on stilts. A balcony ran all the way round it, with steps to the ground. When her eyes got used to the bright sunlight she could see it all clearly.

The South Pole!

There were large pieces of ice floating in the sea and the shore was a mixture of ice-blocks, rocks and brown soil. For a moment Fliss wondered why the ground wasn't covered in snow. Then she realized – it was summer! Of course, she was on the other side of the world. Although summer here was still far colder than any winter at home.

A movement down below grabbed her attention. The earth was shifting. At first she thought it was a trick of the light, but no – the whole shoreline was definitely moving!

Fliss went out on to the balcony. She held tightly to the handrail and leaned forwards, hoping to find out what was happening. Ideas flashed through her mind. Perhaps it was a landslide, or lava oozing from a slow-erupting volcano, or maybe the station was built on drifting ice… She thought about going back inside and using the radios and computers to call for help. But suddenly the wind dropped, the whistling in her ears stopped and the air filled with noise. And it wasn't the creak or crack of land breaking apart. It sounded more like ducks and geese.

Fliss looked again at the moving mass. After a short time, she started to see the tell-tale black and white bodies of … penguins! Lots and lots of penguins! The moving land was a mass of penguins – hundreds, maybe even thousands of them.

She lifted the binoculars to her face, twisting the dials to bring them into focus. Aha, there they were! Sweet black and white penguins, waddling around.

But Fliss didn't want to just look at the birds through binoculars. She wanted to get up close to them. Her heart leaped at the thought of being right there, walking among the penguins of the South Pole.

She ran inside to return the binoculars. As she was coming back out, she noticed a poster on the wall – *Animals of the Antarctic*. Even though it was summer on this side of the world, she'd seen the outside temperature was minus 15. Minus 15! There weren't many animals adapted to that kind of temperature. The poster had pictures of foxes, fishing birds, seals, orcas and – there! – penguins.

There were only four types of penguin that lived this far south: Emperor, Gentoo, Chinstrap and Adélie. Fliss could see right away that these weren't Emperors – she hadn't noticed any blushes of yellow or orange on their chests or necks. This colony had to be one of the other three types. She memorized the pictures so she could identify them when she was up close.

Feeling a bit clumsy in her oversized suit, Fliss carefully made her way down the steps. She was going to meet some penguins – her mum's favourite animal! She felt so warm with happiness that she hardly felt the sting of the freezing air.

Laughing with Penguins

As Fliss walked towards the penguins, their shapes and features became clear. They didn't have the strange markings of Chinstraps, or the wispy white eyebrows of Gentoos. These were Adélie penguins – small, compact and jet-black, apart from their ice-white tummies. She giggled at their funny white-rimmed beady eyes. They were just like the googly eyes she used for her craft projects!

Fliss walked closer, not knowing how they'd react to a human dressed as a giant marshmallow. She expected them to part either side of her, frantic with fear, or flap at her, fiercely protecting their families. But the Adélies were too busy to notice her arrival...

Fliss couldn't see what they were doing at first. It looked as if they were rounding each other up, but soon she saw they were just playing and bickering.

Suddenly, right in front of her, a little Adélie approached a neat heap of stones that another penguin seemed to be guarding. When the guard penguin turned its back, the little penguin quickly snatched up a stone in its beak and waddled away as casually as it could, as if it hadn't done anything wrong.

The guard penguin spotted the pebble-robber and began chasing it at full speed, with its flippers held out and beak open. Fliss imagined it was squawking "thief, thief!" While it was chasing the naughty Adélie, other penguins began to pinch more stones from the unguarded pile. Fliss couldn't help laughing.

She also couldn't understand why
the penguins were so protective of
their stones. It's not as if they were
diamonds and pearls! Besides, they
were everywhere. Looking more closely,
however, Fliss noticed that the pebbles
were stacked in little piles or laid out in
small circles. They were nests! And if
they were nests … there must be chicks!
But Fliss had seen pictures of fluffy
grey and white penguin chicks before,
and there weren't any here.

Just then a penguin waddled so close
to Fliss that it stood on her foot.

"Sorry!" she said. "Did I get in your
way?"

The penguin ignored her, but Fliss
saw a clump of tufty grey feathers on its
otherwise sleek black head.

"Aha! So you *are* chicks," Fliss said. "But your baby feathers have already moulted."

Many of the chicks had lost most of their baby feathers and only had a couple left, sticking out at odd angles on their heads. None of them seemed to have as many as this funny, clumsy penguin. Some had finished moulting altogether, and as the chicks waddled and chased and flapped, the downy feathers drifted around Fliss like a feather storm.

The chick that had stepped on her foot – the one with baby feathers still stuck to its head – waddled back towards her and trod on her foot again.

"Oi! Watch where you're going," teased Fliss.

The little Adélie lifted its neck to look
up at her. It flapped its flippers, made a
short sharp honking noise and scuttled
away again.

Fliss laughed so loudly that the
Adélie stopped and turned round. It
honked again. Was it copying her?
Fliss couldn't stop laughing!

Then she heard another longer, deeper
honk behind her, and Fliss turned to see
an adult penguin running after the little
one. It was having trouble because of a
foot that seemed to be hurt. Its flipper
was damaged too – ripped halfway
down the middle. Fliss wondered what
had happened. Penguins didn't tend
to have land predators and they didn't
usually hurt themselves falling over on
the ice. It must have been something
more serious, like a close shave with a
leopard seal.

The quacking and honking sound of
the colony calmed down and Fliss could
see that more parents had arrived. Most
of them were rounding up their chicks
and guiding them back to the nests.
Nearly all the chicks had two parents

and they huddled together in their stone circles. Something was happening…

Fliss felt the wind suddenly pick up again. To her right, she saw a huge black cloud swiftly approaching and within seconds it was above them. Snowflakes began to fall. Not like they had in her garden, sprinkle-soft. These ones came in sideways and fast. In minutes it was impossible to see anything.

Fliss retreated back to the research station. Penguins were built for this but she wasn't. She could do with a hot drink.

Waddling Away

Inside the station, Fliss found packets
of hot chocolate powder and a kettle.
Just what she needed!

  With hands around her mug, she sat on
a sofa and watched the blizzard through
one of the round windows. She couldn't
see the penguins now, or even the black
mountains. Just the blinding-white gusts
that swirled and swept across the
landscape. And then, as quickly as it had
arrived, the snow was gone.

Fliss jumped up and pressed her nose against the glass.

"Where are you, little Adélie penguins?" she murmured, searching the shore. But it wasn't a waddling mass any more. There was only white. "Where have you gone?"

With a giant quiver, the mass of penguins shook off the snow that clung to their backs, revealing their beautiful dark feathers once again.

Fliss breathed a sigh of relief. For a moment she'd thought they had somehow got swept away, but of course they hadn't.

They were penguins and this was their land. If they could look after themselves so well, then why was she here?

It must have something to do with keeping these Adélies safe, she thought. *But what?*

She didn't have time to think about it for long before a movement down on the shore caught her eye. Not a bustling motion like before. This time it looked as if the colony was forming a line. Fliss watched as they stretched across the landscape, like spilled black paint. The penguins were on the move!

Fliss grabbed the binoculars. The parents were bustling around, steering the chicks ahead of them. This wasn't playtime, it was an organized march. Fliss was so fascinated she was frozen to the spot, even when the silence inside the station was interrupted by the crackle of the communication radio. She made herself listen to the voices. There were two scientists talking. Maybe she would find out why she was here.

"Copy that… The pack ice is completely broken up and coming ashore."

"It's not a surprise. The temperature is way above the norm for this time of year, which means the ice is breaking up. The warm air is bringing rain. A cold front turned it to snow just now – did you see it? Every year it's getting worse. I worry about the penguins."

"They've started their migration north. I've seen three colonies on the move."

"Let's hope they make it past the pack ice."

Fliss, who had been watching the blipping lights on the radio transmitter, turned back to the window. *So that's what's happening*, she thought as the final few penguins left the rock nests down by the shore. *They're migrating!*

Fliss knew that migration was a natural thing to do. Obviously she wasn't here to help them on their way, so maybe she was here for another reason. She was sad about that – she'd have liked to spend longer with the penguins. But while she tried to work out why she *was* here, she decided to go and collect some of the soft grey feathers they had left behind.

She raided the medicine cupboard and found lip balm to stop her lips from cracking. She put on sun cream, too. Although it was freezing, the sun was super bright. With a dry hat and gloves, she stepped out of the research station and walked carefully on the slippery new snow back down to the shore. There had been no snow boots her size at the research station and the treads on her wellies had worn down. With every step she arched back or doubled-over forwards, trying to get her balance. Then she heard the sound of laughter.

Were the scientists back? Were they making fun of her?

She spun round but there was no sign of anyone on the balcony. So where was that sound coming from? There it was again. A honk, this time. It was just like the honk that the clumsy little penguin had made...

It *was* the clumsy little penguin!

Standing alone
in a stone circle,
it stuck out its
neck and honked
again. And again.
The little bird
was calling. All the
others had gone. Fliss felt tears spring
to her eyes – it had been left behind!
She quickly wiped her tears away and
thought about what to do. She could
take the penguin inside and look after it.
But she knew that sometimes it wasn't
good to interfere. She shouldn't do
anything until she understood exactly
what had happened.

She walked up close to the penguin
and crouched down next it. Fliss
remembered her school trip to the zoo

and how she'd learned that chicks could
only be told apart by their calls, and
that male chicks grew larger and fatter
than females. This one was on the small
side, with slightly stumpy flippers and a
short beak, so probably a girl. It cocked
its head to the side and made her smile.

"What are we going to do with you?"
she said to the little penguin.

It honked and waddled closer to
her. Then it backed away. It walked
towards her again and barked in her
face before running off. Fliss laughed
and held out her hand, encouraging it
closer.

"It's OK. I won't hurt you," she
said. "I'm a friendly human. My name
is Fliss and I love animals. What's
your name?"

The penguin made a quacking sound.

"How about I call you Una. It means
'one'. And you really are a special one,
aren't you!"

Fliss reached out her hand further and
stroked Una's soft tummy. An urgent
and angry squawk burst through the
cold air. Fliss turned to see a larger
penguin waddling through the stone
nests, shrieking in annoyance. It was
running as fast as it could, but an

injured leg was slowing it down. It was the mother!

Fliss stood back and allowed the parent penguin to greet her lost child. They must have been separated during the snowstorm. The mother started pushing Una along but Una kept wobbling and stumbling on the stones. Then she fell over. With the mother being so protective, there was nothing Fliss could do. She watched helplessly as they tripped and fell, tripped and fell. In the distance, the last hobbling penguins of the migration pack were barely visible on the horizon. They'd never catch up! Fliss buried her face in her gloved hands and fought back the tears.

Fliss knew she was here to help, but how?

Then she felt something tugging at
her coat. Tug, tug.

Fliss looked down. It was the mother.
She tugged, looked up and put her
head to one side… She was asking for
help! Una fell on her tummy again and
honked twice. It sounded like "ma-ma".

"Of course I'll help you, Mama!"
Fliss said. "Just tell me what to do."

Breaking Ice

Fliss followed Mama over to Una, who'd managed to get up on her feet. Mama butted her along with her soft tummy, but it only made Una wobble and topple over. Fliss could sense Mama's frustration.

"Maybe it would be quicker if I just carried Una for you," she said, placing her hands around the penguin chick.

Una was about the size of Ella's cat, Bodkin, who she picked up a lot. Bodkin

was all wriggling legs and tail but this
felt completely different. Una was like
a smooth, solid rock. She flapped her
flippers as she was lifted up and Fliss
laughed, pulling the little penguin close
to her chest.

"You're built for swimming not flying,
so don't even try!"

Una honked happily, but Mama
wasn't quite so
pleased. She barked
aggressively and
began slapping
Fliss's legs with
her hard flippers.

"OK, OK, I'll put her down," Fliss said calmly, placing Una on the ground.

Mama continued to strut around her and it was hard not to laugh. Even when they were cross, penguins were funny and very sweet. But Fliss knew that animals had different rules of behaviour and she had to respect the rules. Resisting the urge to cuddle animals was going to be one of the hardest things about being a vet! If Mama didn't trust her, Fliss knew she would have to earn that trust. Besides, it was normal for a parent to be protective.

Finally Mama calmed down and stood still. She wasn't showing any signs of trying to catch up with the migrating colony. Fliss wondered if she had changed her mind and decided to

stay at the nesting site. However, it was
nearing the end of summer – winter was
on its way. Without the warmth and
protection of all those other penguins,
how would they survive? Fliss thought
about building them a big nest and
filling it with the moulted feathers, just
to give them the best chance... Then
Mama started walking again.

This time she wasn't heading after the
others. She was making her way towards
the sea. Una flipped and flopped behind
her. Fliss didn't know what to do.

Mama stopped and looked at her. She
honked.

"You want me to come with you?"

Mama honked again.

"All right," Fliss said, smiling with
relief. "I want to help you, I really do."

They stood on the very edge of the shore, where great chunks of pack ice had floated in and stacked up against each other, like giant quartz crystals. It made it hard for a penguin as small as an Adélie to find a quick route into the sea. Mama hopped up on to a piece of ice then on to another one next to it. It had stacked itself at an angle and it was hard for Mama to stand up. Una tried to follow but Mama waddled back, shooing her baby away with her flippers and barking until Una was safely on the shore. Mama tried to get into the sea again.

"You're getting food!" Fliss realized. "Great idea, Mama. Una could do with energy. I'll keep her here, I promise."

Mama hopped forwards – from one

ice block to the next – looking for a way
into the water. Una tried to follow, so
Fliss ran forwards and stood, blocking
her way. Una ran round her. It became a
funny game. Una moved. Fliss blocked.
They ran up and down the shoreline,
honking and laughing.

"I bet you'd be good at chess or Grandmother's Footsteps," Fliss said. "You definitely like playing games, don't you?"

Una tilted her head to one side. *Honk honk!*

"I wonder how your mum's getting on," Fliss said, looking out over the ice. They had moved down the shoreline a little and there was less ice here – just a block or two – and there was a clear view of the sea beyond. Somewhere beneath the surface, Mama was fishing. Fliss shivered at the thought of that ice-cold water as she turned back round.

"Hey, you!"

While Fliss had been gazing out to sea, Una had hopped on to a block of sea ice and flopped down on to her tummy. The little penguin chick slid one way, then used her flippers to rotate her body so she could slide back again. Fliss clapped her hands. Who needs to stand up when you can slide on your belly!

"Clever, Una!" she cried. Una honked back happily.

Suddenly there was a giant *snap!* A *crack!* The noise of grating ice. The ice block was breaking! Una stood up and wobbled as the piece she was standing on broke away and drifted from the shore. Luckily its route out to sea was blocked by ice floes – large sheets of flat ice, but Fliss saw how dangerous the situation could become.

There was another penguin fact she remembered from the zoo – chicks aren't entirely waterproof until they have all their grown-up feathers. Una could freeze if she fell into the ice-cold sea.

"Una!" Fliss shouted. "Don't slide. Don't wobble. I'll come and get you!"

Fliss took off her glove and touched the water beneath the ice blocks. It was so cold it stung her skin. She knew she couldn't get wet in these freezing temperatures without doing herself some damage. And she wouldn't be able to help these penguins if she was hurt.

But what else could she do? Una was drifting further and further out to sea and Mama was still nowhere to be seen.

The Threat of Leopards

The longer Fliss stood not knowing what to do, the less chance there was of saving Una. The ice block had stopped beside another, larger one. It would only take a big wave to split them apart, then Una, stuck on her iceberg island, would move quickly out to sea.

Fliss had to think quickly. She had to think like a vet faced with an emergency and use whatever was available. She had nothing with her that would help save

Una, although there might be things back at the research station.

Fliss turned and started running.

Una honked. It sounded high-pitched and scared.

"I'm coming back, Una, I promise!" Fliss called, waving.

She continued to run as fast as she could, tripping on rocks and skidding on patches of frozen snow that now covered the area. Una's distress calls rang in her ears and Fliss wanted more than anything to comfort the penguin, but she couldn't stop. There wasn't a moment to lose.

The research station was so cosy inside and it would have been lovely to warm up with some hot chocolate. But there was no time for any of that. Instead, Fliss worked fast, rummaging through the cupboards. She had no idea how she was going to rescue Una so she just took anything she thought might be useful. She put it all in a pile in the middle of the floor. A few tins of fish, in case Mama had no luck fishing. Binoculars. Biscuits for energy. A coil of rope. A pickaxe. An aluminium blanket for keeping in body heat. Spare gloves and socks.

There was far too much to stuff in the
pockets of her snowsuit. She spotted
a large backpack hanging on a peg –
perfect! She put the smaller items inside
and tied the pickaxe and her fishing net
to the straps.

Then she ran, slipping and tripping
under the weight of the pack, down to
the shore. Una hadn't drifted far but
the ice blocks that had been keeping
her trapped had moved. Now there
was nothing stopping Una from
drifting out into the ocean. Una was
standing absolutely still and Fliss's
heart thumped to see the baby penguin
looking so alone. She seemed so tiny
against the huge backdrop of the sea
and the towering ice that floated by,
slow, steady and unstoppable.

"I'm here, Una," she called.

Honk honk!

"That's right, Una. Honk honk!" Fliss
shouted cheerily, hoping it would make
the penguin feel better.

Honk honk. Honk. Honk honk honk.

"I'm here, Una!" Fliss called again.
"And I'm going to find a way of

getting you back!"

But Una's honking didn't stop and Fliss could now see a dark shape in the water next to her. Perhaps it was Mama, returned from fishing. Una was probably excited.

Honk honk.

The little penguin's call didn't sound like one of happiness. It was one of alarm. Fliss grabbed the binoculars to get a better look. She twisted the dials to get them in focus and ... now she could see clearly it wasn't Mama in the water. It was a leopard seal. A small one – but even small leopard seals were predators. And this one's sights were set on baby Una.

"Get away from her!" Fliss shouted. "Leave her alone. Hey, seal!"

The leopard seal ignored Fliss's screams as it continued to circle the ice. Una was running from one side of the block to the other in fear. If she fell and slipped off into the sea… Fliss couldn't bear to think about it.

The seal started to heave itself up on to the ice. Fliss looked at the predator again through the binoculars.

The leopard seal was dappled grey and white, its skin as smooth as a pebble. Every time it flung itself on to the ice, it bounced back like a giant water balloon. This was an inexperienced pup and probably hadn't done much hunting – but poor Una didn't know that. She was terrified and her panicky squeals intensified every time the seal came close.

Come on, Fliss, think of something!
Fliss took deep breaths and thought
about the situation. Vets always had to
take animals' feelings into consideration
– and there were two animals in this
situation.

The leopard seal wasn't going to give
up. Why? Because it was hungry. This
animal needed to eat, just like any other.

Of course! Fliss threw the backpack
on the ground and looked inside for the

tinned fish. It was supposed to be for Una to eat. But it was needed right now.

Fliss peeled the lid off one tin and threw the contents into the sea as hard as she could. The chunks of fish fell into the water with a *plop!* right next to the seal. It let go of Una's ice to investigate and guided the sinking fish back to the surface of the water with its flipper. It began to eat. Excellent! Fliss quickly grabbed another tin. This time, she deliberately didn't aim it at the seal. The fish bobbed some way from the ice block before starting to sink. The seal had seen it, though, and followed. Fliss emptied the final tin and threw it way off in another direction, to lure the leopard seal away. The seal slunk under the water and disappeared.

Now she had to get Una back. Who knew how many hungry leopard seals were out there, waiting for a penguin snack? Even though the little penguin wasn't far away, Fliss couldn't go in the water. Somehow she would have to bring the ice back to shore. Fliss looked at the items on the ground where she had thrown the backpack and noticed the rope and the pickaxe. She had an idea.

Fliss put the backpack back on to give her more weight. Then with one end of the rope tied around her tummy and the other around the pickaxe, she lifted and held the pickaxe over her head, waiting for the perfect moment... When Una had moved far enough to one side of the iceberg, out of harm's way, Fliss threw the pickaxe with all her might. It flew through the air, taking a length of rope with it, and struck the ice perfectly.

"That's it, Una! We did it!" Fliss cried happily, pulling the rope carefully so Una didn't fall off the ice block.

She pulled the ice back to the shore and beckoned Una to hop on to the land. But the poor penguin was terrified by her experience and refused to move.

"Come on, little one," Fliss said. "You're safe now." She leaned forwards over the ice to stroke Una and show her everything was OK, but Una shuffled backwards. Fliss leaned further. She would have to grab Una, hold her tightly and hope that Mama didn't get cross.

"Una, I'm your friend – whoops!"

Fliss's footing slipped on the icy wash at her feet. She fell on to the ice block. It rocked under her weight, tipping forwards on the swell of the wave, and then it moved. Out into the water. Out to sea.

Oh no, Fliss thought. *This isn't good at all.*

Slip-Sliding Playtime

When it had just held Una, the ice had looked stable. But now, with Fliss's weight as well, it rocked like an ice cube in fizzy lemonade. Fliss lay absolutely still, but Una was still jumpy from her brush with the leopard seal. She was padding up and down, tilting them backwards and forwards. Fliss knew any big movement would tip them both into the freezing water.

"Hey, Una, it's going to be OK," she

said soothingly, although she wasn't
sure she believed it. They were floating
out to sea – how was everything going
to be OK?

"You'll see," she continued. "It won't
be long until … until…"

Aha! Fliss carefully rose to her feet,
balancing on the block of ice as though
it was a surfboard.

"Until we find a bigger home!" she
finished, wrenching the tip of the
pickaxe free.

Up ahead was a larger block of ice.
It would be like a raft, big enough
for both of them. And although they
weren't exactly home safe and dry,
it would take away the immediate
worry so Fliss could think about what
to do next.

Using her new pick-and-pull method, Fliss threw the pickaxe at the bigger iceberg and dragged their little raft closer to it. Una seemed to understand and sprang to life. Waddling at full speed, she leaped on to the new, bigger iceberg, landing with a *thwack* on her tummy. She started skidding playfully. It was like her very own ice rink!

Fliss stepped across more carefully, fearful of slipping at the last moment as she had done before. Only this time she'd be falling into deep, freezing water.

The ice was thick and sturdy and hardly rocked when Fliss put her weight on it. She stood at the edge, watching her little friend slide around. It reminded her that right now, she should be back home, sliding down the road on plastic bags with Ella. Her brief sadness was brushed away when Una honked a happy *honk*. The penguin was waddling towards her.

"You want me to come and play? OK, Una!"

Fliss stepped forwards but the ice was slippery and she couldn't find a way to stand up straight without wobbling.

"Uh-oh!" she said, feeling her balance go. She jerked forwards, then backwards and then forwards again, falling on to the ice with a big smack. Thank goodness for her puffy snowsuit – without it, she'd be covered in bruises! Una honked and Fliss laughed, unable to stand as her feet slid around like a beginner ice-skater.

Una stood next to her and flapped her flippers. Her honk was more of a cackle now. For a tired little penguin, Una certainly managed to find enough energy to have fun!

"I know I look ridiculous," Fliss said, finally managing to stand upright. Una waddled from side to side on the spot. "You look ridiculous too!"

Then Fliss fell again – *thwack!* – and Una cackled so hard that it became infectious. Soon Fliss was giggling helplessly, which made getting up again impossible. Una circled her, peering at her with curiosity and nuzzling her neck.

When her fit of giggles was over, Fliss stood up. Once again Una waddled on the spot in front of her. Oh … this was a lesson: Una was teaching her how to walk on ice! Fliss watched carefully and copied Una. She leaned forwards so her body weight was right above the front foot. Next, she leaned sideways and brought the back foot alongside the front, moving her body weight across. She did it again. It was slow, but it worked. She was waddling!

"I'm doing it, Una!" Fliss said
gleefully. "I'm walking like a penguin!"

Una showed her pleasure by falling on
to her stomach and skidding across the
ice.

"I'm not doing that!" Fliss laughed,
wobbling slightly as she lost her
concentration. "I'd look more like

a walrus!"

Fliss marvelled at how funny Una could look one minute with her waddling walk, and how graceful she could look the next, gliding as smooth and fast as a bob-sleigh. Up and down the ice she went while Fliss clapped and cheered! And then Una didn't turn in time, perhaps because she was weaker than usual. She slid straight off the edge of the ice and into the sea.

Fliss knew she didn't have time to waddle to the edge – after all, she was still a beginner – so she threw herself on to her stomach and skidded to the place where Una had fallen in. Looking over the edge into the dark blue water, she couldn't see anything. Then Una's little black and white figure appeared beneath

the surface. Fliss waved, signalling
to Una that she was there, and Una
shot out of the water. The leap wasn't
powerful enough to get up on to the ice,
though, and she fell back in.

"Try again, you can do it!" Fliss said.

The penguin flapped her flippers
and propelled herself towards the ice
again. But she was tired – all the playing
around had worn her out. As Una fell
back in, Fliss spotted something else a
few metres away. A flash of black and
white in the water. It was far too big to
be Mama. And it was getting bigger and
bigger.

Oh no!

"Una! You have to hurry!" Fliss
shrieked. "Una! Jump now!"

Fliss looked down at the struggling

penguin and then up again at the
approaching shape. The dorsal fin cut
through the surface, the huge curve of
its back breached the water, black and
shiny. It was an orca – otherwise known
as a killer whale. And it was coming
towards them.

Killer in the Water

Una was weak and there was no time to
hesitate. Two, three seconds at most, is
all it would take for the orca to reach the
ice. And Fliss knew what would happen
to Una if it did.

She yanked off her gloves and plunged
her hands into the water. Pain seared
through her skin, as if it was burning,
but she couldn't give up. If she didn't
save Una she would never be able to
forgive herself.

Clenching her teeth through the pain and pushing away the fear as she felt her hands turning numb, she grabbed the baby penguin. With a yell of might, Fliss pulled her up and out of the water. Holding Una against her chest, she quickly shuffled backwards on her bottom towards the centre of the ice raft, just as the orca's rubbery fin slid by. That was close!

"Are you a-a-a-l-l r-r-right?" Fliss's teeth chattered. There was no happy honk or cackle. The penguin was frozen with fear. "I-I-I'm g-g-oing to put you d-d-down," she stammered.

Fliss placed Una next to her and
fumbled with the backpack. The icy
water had made her hands stop working,
so using her teeth Fliss pulled on
her fleece-lined gloves. As her hands
warmed up and the numbness wore off,
pain ran through her fingers. Although
it hurt, she knew this was a good sign.
It meant her hands weren't damaged
and would soon be working normally
again.

Boom. There was loud bang and the
ice rocked violently. Fliss looked up
to see the orca's fin still alongside the
edge of the iceberg. It had rammed
into it! A cold chill ran up her spine
when she realized what the whale was
doing.

Fliss had seen wildlife documentaries

about killer whales. They were intelligent and they had hunting strategies. They also hunted in groups. She spun round to see if there were others, but the sea was calm and blue. It looked as if this one was on its own. It wouldn't be able to climb on the ice, like the leopard seal, but it had something else in mind. It was going to tip the ice over.

The orca rolled on to its side, revealing how big it was. Its enormous fin pointed skywards, like a towering mountain. It rolled back again, smacking the water and creating an almighty wave that rocked the iceberg backwards. The pack ice had felt so strong before, but now it was being tossed about like a dingy on a rough sea. The orca rolled on to its side once more.

"Una, stand up, don't lie down," Fliss said, knowing that if they lost their balance they would slip off the ice and into the sea. "I need to make a safe place for us."

Una had been screeching and flapping when the seal was around, but now she was very tired and frightened. She certainly wasn't in the mood to play slip-slide on her tummy. She stood on her flat feet and shuffled about nervously as Fliss set to work with the pickaxe. She dug at a point in the centre of the ice. If she could make a hole for them to sit in, they wouldn't be thrown off so easily, and perhaps the orca would lose interest. Fliss wasn't sure if it would work, but it was the only chance they had. She chipped away at the ice.

The orca made another massive wave. Fliss yelled and with one hand she held on to the axe, which she had just dug into the ice, and with the other she grabbed Una's flipper. Phew! But they might not be so lucky next time.

"Quick, Una," Fliss said, pulling the penguin into the hole she had dug. "Sit in here."

The orca slammed the ice again, but though Fliss had managed to get Una safely into the hole, she slipped. Her legs slid out from underneath her, but she just managed to grip the edge of the hole as her body slid down the ice.

The ice settled and when Fliss looked up, the orca was gone. Her heart was beating like a drum, her mouth was dry and her lungs were burning from

breathing fast in the cold, cold air. She
shakily slid herself to the edge of the
ice and looked out over the water. The
huge dark shape of the orca was finally
moving away.

Fliss sat up and watched it go,
breathing a sigh of relief. Una waddled
up to her and stood close. She seemed
to understand that Fliss needed to see a
friendly face.

Honk!

"Oh, Una," Fliss said. "That was
close, wasn't it?"

Honk! Honk!

Fliss stroked the little penguin's head,
noticing that the few chick feathers that
still clung to it were soaking wet. Some
were even forming ice crystals. Fliss
fetched a towel from her backpack and

rubbed Una's
head until all the
water was gone.

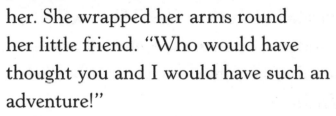

"Come here,
fuzzy head," she
said affectionately,
pulling Una towards
her. She wrapped her arms round
her little friend. "Who would have
thought you and I would have such an
adventure!"

They sat together quietly, looking out
to sea, catching their breath.

Now that the drama was over, Fliss
couldn't help thinking how lucky she
had been. Not just to survive, but to
actually see a killer whale in the wild!
Fliss had never thought she'd get to see
one. And now she had – the smooth

marble of its white tummy and its
jet-black back, and even its beady
eyes. It was incredible. Although she
thought that one close encounter with a
killer whale was probably enough for a
lifetime!

But then she saw a ripple on the
surface beyond the ice. There was
something else in the water. A smaller
creature this time – dark, with a flash
of white.

Learning to Fish

It was Mama! When she spotted Una she came zooming towards the ice as fast as she could. She shot out of the sea and landed next to Fliss.

"Well done, Mama," said Fliss, crying with relief. She held out her arms to take the poor, terrified penguin in a hug. But Mama was up on her feet, slapping Fliss away. She wanted to see her child. Fliss was heartened to see that Mama's injuries didn't get in the way of her survival instinct. Or her determination.

Mama rushed up to Una and brushed her neck against the little penguin, but she didn't open her beak wide or lower her head. It was clear she hadn't found any food, though it was not surprising as the sea was full of predators. It was a miracle she'd actually made it back alive. Now Una needed something to give her energy, quickly. Fliss wished she hadn't used all the tinned fish to lure away the leopard seal.

Suddenly Mama looked alert and waddled to the edge of the ice. She had spotted something. Fliss hoped it wasn't another killer whale – she didn't know if she had the energy to save them all again. But Mama didn't honk with alarm. Instead, she turned to Fliss and flapped her flippers. Then she turned back to face the water.

"What can you see, Mama?" Fliss said, penguin-waddling as carefully as she could to the edge.

Ahead of them, a smoky pink cloud bloomed in the dark blue waters of the sea. As the pink patch floated closer, Fliss saw that it was made up of very small creatures. Teeny tiny shrimps. Millions of them. Krill!

"It's food, Mama!" Fliss cried happily. However, getting back in the water wasn't something Mama was keen to do, not with sharp-toothed predators lurking below the surface. Fliss looked at her pile of equipment. Her fishing net was still tied to the backpack. "I have an idea," she said.

The holes in her fishing net were far too large though, and the krill slipped through, and Mama soon lost interest in Fliss's attempts at fishing. She waddled back to where Una was sitting in the hole. She nudged Una out and started pecking at the ice, making the hole deeper. Fliss didn't know what she was doing, but she did know that Mama had strong survival instincts. She watched as the big penguin pecked hard at the ice. If she kept on going, she'd break through!

Fliss gasped. "That's what you're trying to do! You're making a fishing hole! Let me help."

Mama was bossy and kept flipper-slapping Fliss as she tried to get to the hole. Eventually Fliss nudged her aside and was able to quickly finish the job with her pickaxe. They stood together in the middle of the floating ice, looking through the hole at the sea beneath. Occasionally waves lapped up through it. The bloom of krill was getting closer and it wouldn't be much longer until it was right beneath the iceberg.

Mama and Una would have all the food they needed to restore their energy without the danger of a deep-sea dive.

Although their troubles weren't over yet, Fliss allowed herself a moment of rest. She sat down, ate a couple of biscuits and swapped her ice-encrusted gloves with the spare ones she had packed. Then she watched, tired and happy, as her friendly penguins filled themselves on krill. Mama would stick her head into the hole, gobble up a load of shrimp, and drop it into Una's wide-open mouth. It certainly wasn't the most pleasant thing to watch, but Fliss knew it was all part of nature: a mother feeding her young.

Within minutes both Una and Mama
were looking brighter. When they
had finished eating, Mama did an
almighty shake, spraying water droplets
everywhere. After that, she looked as
dry as if she'd never plunged into the
sea. Una, however, was shivering. With
the water dripping from Mama, and
the sea spray that showered them every
time the water lapped at the ice, Una
was finding it hard to stay dry. She was
starting to freeze.

History Lessons

Fliss wrapped the aluminium blanket
round Una, but it wasn't soft and
floppy like a normal blanket and it
wouldn't stay on the chick's shoulders
without Fliss holding it there. That
wasn't something Mama was keen on
– she cuddled up close to her baby,
smothering her with her chest feathers.
It wasn't enough – Una was still shaking
with cold. Mama looked up at Fliss and
shuffled round a bit. She was making

room for her!

Feeling honoured, Fliss huddled with the penguins, glad to be able to give them a little more warmth. But if the temperature dropped any further or if they ended up in the water again, they'd be in trouble. Fliss needed to get them back on land and find help.

"Hold tight. I'm just going to look for ice floes."

The shore on which the New Captain Scott Research Station stood was now far behind them – they had drifted some way on their iceberg. Rather than fighting the flow of the ocean, Fliss knew that their best chance of survival was to get on to the nearest shore and walk. There was a headland up ahead of them, and plenty of floating ice to use as stepping stones to get there.

Fliss stepped forwards and slipped, sprawling on the ice like a starfish. She briefly imagined Kamal laughing at her and suddenly felt very far from home. She pushed the thought away. She could worry about that when she got these penguins to safety. That's clearly what she was here to do.

In the meantime, if she was going to be moving across the ice at speed, throwing and pulling the pickaxe, the skidding was definitely going to be a problem. So she set about chipping little holes across the iceberg to break up the surface and give her places where she could dig in the toes of her boots. Una and Mama huddled together and watched. Now that Fliss had helped with the fishing hole, it seemed Mama trusted her a little more.

With her pickaxe, Fliss pulled the first chunk of ice towards them. "Come on," she said, heaving the backpack over her shoulder. "Follow me."

She stepped carefully on to the next block and waited for the penguins to follow. Despite being so cold, Una flopped down on her tummy and skidded playfully across on to the new ice floe.

"Steady now!" Fliss laughed. "You don't want to fall in the water again. Your turn, Mama!"

Fliss and Una stood on the iceberg and waited for Mama. But Mama hadn't seen Fliss's pick-and-pull method of getting across the ice before and hesitated, honking angrily at them as if they were naughty children. When she realized that Una wasn't coming back, she reluctantly waddled across.

"You're going to have to be quicker than that," Fliss said, shaking her head. "We've got a long way to go."

Carefully, steadily, Fliss created icy stepping stones and they made their way across the bay to the headland. The ice wasn't so stacked up here and they managed to reach the shore without difficulty, although Una was very weak. It was only her playful nature that kept her going. She was shuddering with the cold and her movements were becoming jerky. Fliss was about to pick her up, despite Mama's protectiveness, when she saw a solid shape in the distance.

"There's a building over there!" Fliss cried. "Maybe it's another research station. They'll be able to help! Come on, Una. Come on, Mama. Keep going!"

But the building wasn't a research station. Fliss wanted to cry as she saw its old wooden walls – it was just a hut! Dragging her feet, she walked up to it and wiped the ice from a plaque on the wall. *Shackleton's Hut.*

"Another explorer." She sighed. "It

was an amazing bit of history, but that doesn't help us much, does it? Come on, let's go inside and see if there's anything that isn't rotten."

Fliss pushed open the door. The hut was surprisingly cosy. The sunlight that streamed through the window had warmed the air inside. There were blankets and mattresses. There were tins of food on the shelves. It was old, but it was perfectly intact. Fliss laughed with relief and quietly thanked Ernest Shackleton and his adventurers for building such a sturdy hut. Now she had to get the penguins comfortable and dry, which was hard when Mama was still so protective. Poor Mama. She probably never dreamed she'd be teaming up with a human that looked like a puffy yeti! Fliss took off her giant snowsuit and saw the penguins' curious faces as she halved in size.

"Yep, this is me," Fliss laughed. "Much smaller in real life!"

Concerned about the freezing temperatures, Fliss's first job was to make sure that they all recovered from their adventures out on the water. Mama had given herself a big shake, but Una was looking a bit bedraggled. Fliss found an old blanket and rubbed the little penguin down until she was totally dry. They were all safe. For now.

Fliss was suddenly overcome with tiredness. Her arms were exhausted from lifting the pickaxe, her entire body ached from the cold that had crept through the puffy layers of her snowsuit, and her mind was strained from being alert for hours.

What time is it? she wondered. It was still bright outside, but her eyes felt heavy as if it were evening time.

She remembered that at the North
and South Poles it was impossible to
time your days by sunrise and sunset. In
summer they had six months of sun and
in winter six months of darkness. Now
Fliss didn't know whether to let herself
fall asleep or stay awake! She smiled at
Una and Mama, who were snuggling
against each other tightly, and thought
of her own parents. She missed them.
She missed home... How would she
get back there? Why was she still here?
If it was to rescue these sweet Adélie
penguins, her job was done, wasn't it?

There must be something else she had
to do.

To stop herself from falling asleep,
Fliss got up and looked for some food.
There were still some oat biscuits left

over in her backpack. She ate them as she paced around the hut, searching for clues.

There was a book on the table. It was open at a page with spiky handwriting. The ink had faded and it was hard to read, but Fliss saw that it was dated 1917 – over a hundred years ago! It was a diary entry by one of the men on Shackleton's expedition, perhaps even Shackleton himself. It talked of the stress and loneliness of being at the South Pole. Fliss recognized some of the descriptions and feelings, and she decided that if even these strong explorers found it difficult then she had been very brave indeed. And she was definitely capable of being a vet in all situations!

There was another section to the diary entry. It described the Adélie penguin migration. The writer said he had watched it pass by this very hut – thousands and thousands of penguins!

"Wow!" Fliss said aloud. "For centuries the migrations have been taking place right here, following in the footsteps of the generations of penguins before them…"

Fliss looked across at her two beautiful penguins, who were looking back at her, blinking in the stream of sunlight through the window.

"Migration is in your blood, it's part of your life. *This* is my task, isn't it?" It was more of a realization than a question and Fliss nodded at her friends. "I need to reunite you with your colony. You have to join the migration!"

But how?

Joining the Migration

Fliss looked through the journal for more details. All she could find out was that the Adélies went north at the end of summer to a warmer climate and better feeding grounds. There had to be something else in Shackleton's hut that could help her. But the hut was old and she could only see books and scrolls of paper.

Fliss unrolled a scroll. The paper was yellowed and crinkly and she had to pin it to the table with a kettle and a cup to stop it curling up again. It was a map of Ross Island. Shackleton had marked the position of his hut with a box and his name scrawled above it.

If the Adélie colony that the writer had seen had started their migration outside Captain Scott's old hut, there was a good chance that Una and Ma's colony would be taking the same route. If they were, they'd be passing Shackleton's hut. Perhaps they had done so already. If they had, there would be footprints in the earth and in the snow...

Fliss ran outside. No footprints. Was it possible that they had crossed the bay on their ice floes faster than the penguins could walk? Maybe, just maybe, they were in the right place at the right time!

Then, carried on the thin air, came a cacophony of honking, like a distant traffic jam. Fliss stared until dots danced in front of her eyes. She blinked. They weren't dots. They were penguins!

"It's the front of the migration line," she gasped.

Fliss ran back into the hut, a huge grin on her face. "Quick, Mama, your colony is coming. Quick, quick!"

The penguins sensed Fliss's excitement and started waddling around the hut crazily like bouncy balls. Fliss took the opportunity to give Una a last rub down with the towel – she needed to be in the best condition to tackle the migration ahead of her. As the towel dropped to the floor, so did the last of

Una's baby feathers. In front of Fliss stood a sleek, black and white, fully waterproof chick.

"You're perfect," Fliss said, a tear springing to her eye. "Hey!"

Mama was bustling around Fliss's legs, but this time her flippers weren't beating her back. Instead, they were pushing Una forwards between her legs. Fliss sniffed back her tears and laughed as Una snuggled in, and Mama, now completely trusting, wrapped her flippers round Fliss's shins. They stood like that for a minute and Fliss savoured every moment of the group hug. She knew this was goodbye. Once Una and Mama had joined the colony, her time with the playful Adélie chick and her incredible, brave mother would be over.

"We've been through so much together! It's hard to leave you," Fliss said. "But you need to be with your colony. And I need to be with mine."

Mama gave a gentle honk and stepped back, leaving Fliss and Una to share one last cuddle together.

"You too now, Una," Fliss said, gulping back tears. "You're going to be just fine."

Through the window, the first bobbing heads of the migrating penguins came into view and the sound of squabbles and squawks grew louder. Una rocked from side to side. Perhaps she could hear her friends. Fliss smiled as she remembered seeing them all that first time, stealing stones and chasing each other. It seemed like so long ago when it had actually all been the same day ... or at least, she thought it had!

Fliss opened the door. Laughter replaced the tears as hundreds of Adélies trudged past, chattering loudly. She had a deep respect for penguins now that she'd spent some time with them, but they were still so funny!

"Go now," Fliss said. "Shoo!"

Mama slapped her leg with a flipper, but it wasn't a telling-off. It was a last show of contact before she continued north. Una scuttled after her. Outside, the funny chick turned and looked at Fliss once more before joining the crowd.

Fliss kept her eyes on Una for as long as possible – on the little penguin who had survived against all the odds, who loved to slide on her tummy and whose mother would protect her until she was grown up.

Eventually Fliss lost sight of her among the thousands of penguins. But she stood at the door of the hut and stared into the distance long after they'd disappeared over the rocky hill.

"Bye bye!" she called. "Hope you live happily ever after. Or Adélie ever after!" That sounded like something Ella would say!

Fliss wondered if Ella had finished her breakfast and was waiting for her back home… Without the penguins, the South Pole was a very lonely place.

The wind picked up and began to whip snow and ice crystals through the air. Fliss's face stung and without her snowsuit she started to feel very cold. She stepped back into Shackleton's hut and shut the door. In respect for the great explorer that had provided her with shelter, she decided to tidy up the hut. Then she would walk back to the New Captain Scott Research Station. If the old map was right, all she had to do was follow the shore southwards. If she couldn't get home any other way, she'd just have to radio for help or sit and wait for one of the scientists to come back.

There was a bang on the door. The wind, maybe? Then came another bang. Followed by another.

Someone was out there. And whoever it was, they weren't giving up.

Adélies in the Garden

Fliss's heart thumped. Should she answer the door and ask for help? Perhaps she'd be in trouble for entering a historical site without permission! Should she hide? But if she hid, they might go away, and this could be her only chance to get help and find a way home...

Fliss walked to the door and placed her hand on the handle. She looked once more around the hut that had provided shelter and warmth and saved the lost Adélie penguins. Then she opened the door.

There was a *whoosh* of cold air and
Fliss had to shut her eyes against the
blast of snow. The storm must have
closed in very quickly. When she wiped
the snow from her eyes a familiar face
was staring at her.

"Gotcha!"

In front of her, Ella was doing a
victory dance.

"Ella!" Fliss exclaimed, stepping out
into the cold.

"Don't complain, it was only a little
snowball to say hi. Come on, you
and I need to get to work. Kamal and
Alisha have declared snow war. We
need to be prepared. Have you got a
wheelbarrow in there or anything we
can use to collect snow?"

Confused, Fliss looked behind her, back into Shackleton's hut. Only it wasn't an expedition hut any more. It was a dusty old shed full of plant pots and tools. She was home. Fliss tipped back her head and laughed and laughed.

"What's so funny?" Ella said.

"Incoming!" Kamal's voice shouted.

Ella jumped to the side and Fliss was peppered with the neighbours' snowball ambush, including one right on the nose.

"Sorry, Fliss!" Kamal said sincerely.

"Sorry!" Alisha echoed. "I'll tell my brother not to do that again."

But Fliss was still laughing. "That's OK, Alisha. A little snow never hurt anyone. Besides, it's good experience. Who knows when I might find myself helping an animal stranded in the Antarctic!"

"You'll never move that far away," Ella said huffily.

"Why not – don't you think I'm strong enough?" Fliss challenged, crossing her arms.

"Of course you are. I just wouldn't let you go. I'd miss you too much, that's all."

"I missed you too, Ella," Fliss smiled, ignoring her friend's confused face. "Now, let's come up with a plan to get

Kamal back!"

Ella and Fliss spent all morning and afternoon having snowball fights and slip-slide races down the road, only stopping when Ella wanted to go inside and warm up. Fliss felt fine. It was cold, but it wasn't *that* cold!

When the sun began to set at four o'clock, it took Fliss by surprise. She had been in daylight for so long, she had forgotten how the snow glowed an eerie blue when the light faded, and how the temperature dropped when the sun disappeared.

"I hope it snows again tonight," said Ella.

"Me too," Fliss agreed. "But we should build something to celebrate today, just in case it doesn't."

"A snowman? Great idea!" Ella said, starting to gather snow together in a heap. Fliss watched her for a while.

"Why don't we do something a bit different?" she suggested. "Like a snow penguin."

"Yeah, a penguin. A big Emperor penguin!"

"Or how about an Adélie penguin instead?" Fliss said. "They're small and super cute."

In the dying light, Fliss and Ella built up their heap of snow and smoothed it down, carving out feet and flippers and shaping a head. They created a beak with strips of bark. Ella waddled around it, chanting "Snow, snow, penguino" and Fliss laughed and stroked the frozen statue until it was as smooth as a real penguin.

She stood back and looked at it,
beaming with pride and feeling emotional
as it brought back memories of Una and
Mama and their great adventure on the ice
floes of the Antarctic. Fliss would never
be a famous name alongside Scott and
Shackleton, but in a way she had made her
mark on the South Pole – she had made
sure that two Adélie penguins lived to
continue their story.

"Hey, what's that?"

Alisha was peering over the fence. Kamal popped up next to her.

"It's an Indian penguin," Ella said proudly.

"An Indian penguin?" Alisha laughed. "There's no such thing."

"Well, that's what Fliss says and Fliss knows everything about animals."

"I never said it was an Indian penguin, Ella!" Fliss said. "Penguins only live in the southern hemisphere. India is in the northern hemisphere."

"But you said it was a Delhi penguin, and everyone knows Delhi is in India."

When Fliss realized Ella's mistake, she burst out laughing and soon the others were laughing too, although they didn't know why.

"Adélie. It's an *Adélie* penguin, not *a Delhi* penguin!" Fliss gasped, when she could speak again.

"Adélie!" Ella slapped her hand across her face. "I'm such a banana!"

After hot dogs for tea, Ella's mum came to pick her up. She and Fliss hugged and crossed their fingers that there'd be two snow days in a row.

When Ella had gone, Fliss ran upstairs and changed into her pyjamas and fluffy slippers. It felt so good to be comfortable and warm again. She snuggled up on the sofa with a mug of hot chocolate and watched a documentary about beehives. But she couldn't stop thinking about Una. She got up and pressed her nose against the window.

The garden glistened in the moonlight – all white, blue and black. Her eyes were drawn to the Adélie penguin. Thanks to the freezing air, it was still perfect. But next to it was another mound of snow. Fliss frowned. Hmmm… What could it be?

Fliss opened the back door and stepped out into the night.

It wasn't a mound of snow… It was another penguin! Smaller, but just as perfect. Oh goodness, it was Mama and Una. Fliss stared and stared, hardly believing what she was seeing.

She stayed there until the mug of hot chocolate in her hands had gone cold and the snow had begun melting through the soles of her fluffy slippers.

"It was lovely to see you again. But I've got to go."

She turned to go back inside. Before she closed the door, she looked once again at her Adélie friends and smiled.

"Time to migrate. Don't be late," she whispered.

Snow Una's eyes twinkled back at her like diamonds.

Maybe it was just the moonlight dancing on the snow crystals. Or maybe it was a playful penguin chick saying a last goodbye.

Rachel Delahaye was born in Australia but has lived in the UK since she was six years old. She studied linguistics and worked as a magazine writer and editor before becoming a children's author. She loves words and animals; when she can combine the two, she is very happy indeed! At home, Rachel loves to read, write and watch wildlife documentaries. Outside, she loves to go walking in woodland. She also follows news about animal rights and the environment and hopes that one day the world will be a better home for all species, not just humans!

Rachel has two lively children and a dog called Rocket, and lives in the beautiful city of Bath.